Catch It, Jess!
and
Cat Nap

'Catch It, Jess!' and 'Cat Nap'
An original concept by Katie Dale
© Katie Dale

Illustrated by Kasia Dudziuk
© Kasia Dudziuk

Published by MAVERICK ARTS PUBLISHING LTD

Studio 3A, City Business Centre, 6 Brighton Road,

Horsham, West Sussex, RH13 5BB

© Maverick Arts Publishing Limited May 2018

+44 (0)1403 256941

A CIP catalogue record for this book is available at the British Library.

ISBN 978-1-84886-348-4

Maverick

www.maverickbooks.co.uk

Red

This book is rated as: Red Band (Guided Reading)
This story is decodable at Letters and Sounds Phase 2.

Catch It, Jess!
and
Cat Nap

By **Katie Dale**
Illustrated by **Kasia Dudziuk**

The Letter E

Trace the lower and upper case letter with a finger. Sound out the letter.

*Across,
around*

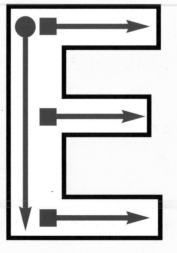

*Down,
lift, cross,
lift, cross,
lift, cross*

Some words to familiarise:

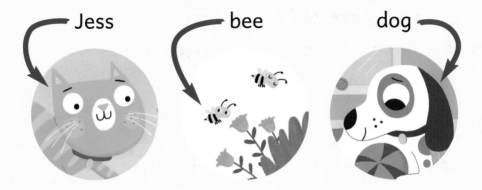

Jess   bee   dog

High-frequency words:

a   on   the   it   no   he   her

Tips for Reading 'Catch It, Jess!'

- Practise the words listed above before reading the story.

- If the reader struggles with any of the other words, ask them to look for sounds they know in the word. Encourage them to sound out the words and help them read the words if necessary.

- After reading the story, ask the reader if they remember whether Jess could catch anything.

Fun Activity

Can you think of any other animals Jess could chase?

Catch It, Jess!

Jess spots a black rat on the log.

Run, Jess! Can she catch it?

No!

Jess spots a fat duck on the rock.

Run, Jess! Can she catch it?

No!

Jess spots a buzzing bee on the tree.

Run, Jess!
Can she catch it?

No!

Jess spots a red ball on the hill.

Run, Jess! Can she catch it?

No!

Jess spots a big dog
on the mat.

14

Run, Jess! Can he catch her?

The Letter A

Trace the lower and upper case letter with a finger. Sound out the letter.

Around,
up,
down

Down,
up,
down,
lift,
cross

Some words to familiarise:

hens   frogs   Nan

High-frequency words:

on a go the

Tips for Reading 'Cat Nap'

- Practise the words listed above before reading the story.

- If the reader struggles with any of the other words, ask them to look for sounds they know in the word. Encourage them to sound out the words and help them read the words if necessary.

- After reading the story, ask the reader why Jess could not nap.

Fun Activity

Ask the reader if they know anyone that snores!

Cat Nap

Jess sits on a bench.

"Buzz!" go the bees.

Sh, bees!

Jess cannot nap here.

Jess sits on a step.

Jess sits on a log.

"Ribbit!" go the frogs.

Sh, frogs!

Jess cannot nap here.

Jess sits on a rock.

"Quack!" go the ducks.

Sh, ducks!

Jess cannot nap here.

Jess sits on Nan's lap.

Jess can nap.

But Nan cannot nap!

Book Bands for Guided Reading

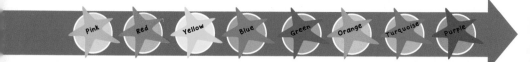

Red

Dog in a Dress and Run, Tom, Run!	Buzz and Jump! Jump!	Bam-Boo and I Wish	Sam the Star and Clown Fun!	Seeds and Stuck in the Tree
978-1-84886-290-6	978-1-84886-250-0	978-1-84886-251-7	978-1-84886-288-3	978-1-84886-289-0
Viv the Vet and Top Dog	Go Away! and Let's Make A Rocket	Catch It, Jess! and Cat Nap	Grandad's Cake and Grandad's Pot	Zoom! and Come Back, Mack!
978-1-84886-347-7	978-1-84886-350-7	978-1-84886-348-4	978-1-84886-351-4	978-1-84886-349-1

Plus many more titles in the scheme!

To view the whole Maverick Readers scheme, please visit:

www.maverickbooks.co.uk/early-readers

The Institute of Education book banding system is a scale of colours that reflects the various levels of reading difficulty. The bands are assigned by taking into account the content, the language style, the layout and phonics.

Maverick Early Readers are a bright, attractive range of books covering the pink to purple bands. All of these books have been book banded for guided reading to the industry standard and edited by a leading educational consultant.